# Alfie and the
# Birthday Surprise

**Other books about Alfie:**

*All About Alfie*

*The Big Alfie and Annie Rose Storybook*

*The Big Alfie Out of Doors Storybook*

*Rhymes for Annie Rose*

First published 1997 in Great Britain by
The Bodley Head Children's Books, Random House
First U.S. edition published 1998 by Lothrop, Lee & Shepard Books
an imprint of Morrow Junior Books
a division of William Morrow and Company, Inc.
1350 Avenue of the Americas, New York, NY 10019

Printed in Hong Kong by South China Printing Company (1988) Ltd.

1 3 5 7 9 10 8 6 4 2

Library of Congress Cataloging-in-Publication Data
Hughes, Shirley.
Alfie and the birthday surprise / Shirley Hughes.
p. cm.
Summary: The death of Bob's cat prompts his friends and family to
give him a surprise birthday party and a very special present.
ISBN 0-688-15187-6
[1. Cats—Fiction.  2. Death—Fiction.  3. Birthdays—Fiction.
4. Parties—Fiction.]  I. Title.  PZ7.H87395Af 1998
[E]—dc21  97-6472  CIP  AC

# ALFIE
### and the

## BIRTHDAY SURPRISE

*Shirley Hughes*

LOTHROP, LEE & SHEPARD BOOKS • MORROW
NEW YORK

Alfie lived in the city with his mom and dad and his little sister, Annie Rose. Right across the street lived their good friends the MacNallys. There were Bob and Jean MacNally, their daughter, Maureen, and their old cat, Smoky.

Every morning, when Maureen set off for school and Bob MacNally went to catch his bus to work, they waved to Alfie and Annie Rose, and Alfie and Annie Rose waved back.

Smoky was always there to see them off. And on fine evenings he would sit on the wall for a long time, waiting for them to come back. Alfie's cat, Chessie, and Smoky were not good friends. They eyed each other suspiciously from opposite sides of the street. But Bob MacNally told Alfie that Smoky was getting too old to pick fights.

The MacNallys were
all very fond of Smoky,
but Bob and he were
special friends. When
Bob came home from
work, he always stopped
for a chat with Smoky.

Once, when Smoky was frightened up a tree and got stuck,
Bob spent a whole afternoon trying to coax him down. "It's
his back legs, you see," Bob told Alfie. "I'm afraid he's not as
young as he used to be."

Smoky spent most of his days asleep in his favorite place by the kitchen radiator or dozing in a patch of sunlight.

But in the evenings he would jump into Bob MacNally's lap, and they would watch television together.

Smoky never wanted to play. When Alfie was visiting the MacNallys, he would try pulling a piece of string across the floor and twitching the end, hoping that Smoky would chase after it. But Smoky only opened one slit of an eye, cocked his ears halfheartedly, and went back to sleep.

If Alfie picked him up, he made bad-tempered noises that meant he wanted to be left alone.

Smoky just wanted to sleep . . . and sleep. . . .

One morning Maureen came over to Alfie's house before breakfast. She was very sad. She told them that Smoky had died in the night.

"He was almost as old as I am," Maureen told them tearfully. "And that's pretty old for a cat!"

Alfie was sad about Smoky being dead. "We won't see him again, will we?" he said to Mom. "Why does Smoky have to be dead?" he wanted to know.

"Well, he was very old and tired, and he had come to the end of his life," said Mom. "But it was a happy life, and we'll always remember him."

Smoky was buried under a bush in the MacNallys'
backyard. Maureen made a memorial for him in her
woodworking class at school. Alfie helped her put it up.

She had written on it in beautiful writing:

In memory of
SMOKY
A good friend

They all cried over it, and then they began to feel better.
All except Bob. Smoky had been his special friend, and
he missed him a lot, especially in the evenings when he
came home from work and there was no Smoky waiting
on the wall.

"It's Dad's birthday next week," Maureen told Mom and Alfie when she was sitting in their kitchen one afternoon. "He'll be fifty-two. And he says he doesn't want any presents at all. Not even cards."

"Not even balloons?" asked Alfie.

"No, nothing. He is really down," said Maureen gloomily. "And Mom says she doesn't know what to do to cheer him up."

"He's missing Smoky, I expect," said Mom.

Then Alfie said, "Let's make a party for him!"

Everyone thought that was a wonderful idea. But they decided to keep it a secret until the day came. A surprise birthday party for Bob MacNally!

"When we go shopping, you can choose a present for him," Mom told Alfie.

They looked at a great many things until they decided on a handsome pair of red socks, Alfie's favorite color. Mom bought a box of mint chocolates and some pretty wrapping paper.

The party was such a big secret that Jean MacNally came
over to Alfie's house especially to make the birthday cake
in their kitchen. Alfie helped her put on the candles—five
blue ones and two pink ones.

The day before the surprise
party, all Bob's presents were
ready. Jean had knitted him
a sweater.

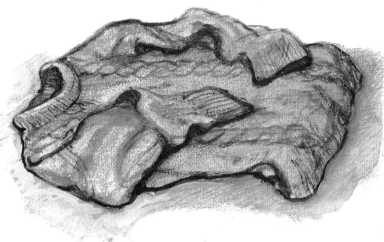

Mom and Dad had bought him
a potted plant, and Annie Rose
was giving him a pitcher with a
picture of the sun, moon, and
stars on it.

"What's your present?" Alfie
asked Maureen. But she just
looked mysterious and said
she wasn't telling, not yet.
   "I'll let you know this
evening," she promised.

Annie Rose was already asleep and Alfie was in his
bathrobe, having a story, when Maureen rang the
doorbell. She was carrying a basket tied up with string.
"Is that the present?" asked Alfie, very excited.
"Yes. You can look inside if you like," said Maureen.

She put the basket down carefully in the middle of the floor and undid the string. Then she lifted the lid just a tiny bit. Alfie looked inside.

It was something alive! He saw two very bright eyes and a pink nose with white whiskers.

Then a soft paw shot out and patted his finger.

"Oh, Maureen, it's a kitten," said Mom.

"I got him from a friend at school," said Maureen, beaming. "Will you look after him till tomorrow? It's got to be a real surprise."

"Oh, YES!" shouted Alfie.

Mom said that they could, since it was just for one night. "But we'll have to be careful that Chessie doesn't meet him or she might be jealous," she told Alfie.

"The kitten can sleep in my room," said Alfie.

That night Alfie and the kitten settled down together. Or tried to settle down. It wasn't very easy because the kitten kept batting the edge of Alfie's quilt and trying to climb up it. Then he got onto the bed and started a game of hide-and-seek.

At last he curled up and went to sleep. Alfie loved feeling him at the end of his bed. But he would not have wanted him there every night.

The next day, after Bob had gone to work, they were very busy going back and forth across the street and getting the party ready. Alfie and Maureen fed the kitten and put him in his basket. They hid him in the little room where the MacNallys kept their washing machine. At first the kitten did not like being in there.

"Don't worry—it won't be for long," whispered Alfie. Soon the kitten stopped scratching and was quiet.

At six o'clock everything was ready. They turned off
the lights and waited in the dark. At last they heard
Bob coming up the front steps.

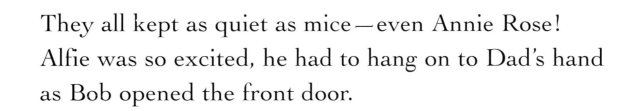

They all kept as quiet as mice—even Annie Rose!
Alfie was so excited, he had to hang on to Dad's hand
as Bob opened the front door.

"Hello? I'm home!" he called. Silence. Then he walked
into the living room. On went the lights, and they all burst
out singing, "Happy birthday to you!" At first Bob was so
surprised, he just stood there with his eyes and mouth
wide open. Then he began to smile.

He was very pleased with his birthday party and his presents.

He opened them all, one by one.

But best of all was when Maureen, helped by Alfie,
brought in the basket. Bob untied the string and
out jumped the kitten! Right away he started a
game with Bob's shoelaces.

Bob MacNally called the kitten Boots.

Boots was wonderfully good at inventing games. When Alfie pulled a piece of crumpled paper across the floor, Boots lay in wait for it and then pounced.

He tossed it in the air and bicycled on it furiously with his little back legs.

Alfie showed Annie Rose how to play with Boots and
how not to squeeze him too hard.

Boots soon settled down as one of the MacNally family,
and Bob grew very fond of him. Though, of course,
they never forgot dear old Smoky.

Alfie and Boots became great friends. Alfie was quite
sure that Boots remembered how once, before Bob
MacNally's surprise birthday party, he had slept a whole
night on the end of Alfie's bed.